DAT DUE

Dance

★ ★ ★ ★ ★

A PRACTICAL GUIDE TO PURSUING THE ART

★ ★ ★ ★ ★

BY REBECCA LOVE FISHKIN

CONTENT ADVISER
Hannah Seidel, Dancer, Gibney Dance,
Erica Essner Performance Co-op, and Chris Ferris and Dancers

READING ADVISER
Alexa L. Sandmann, EdD, Professor of Literacy,
College and Graduate School of Education, Health, and Human Services,
Kent State University

COMPASS POINT BOOKS
a capstone imprint

Compass Point Books
151 Good Counsel Drive
P.O. Box 669
Mankato, MN 56002-0669

Printed in the United States of America in Stevens Point, Wisconsin.
032010
005741WZF10

Editor: Jennifer Fretland VanVoorst
Designer: Ashlee Suker
Media Researcher: Svetlana Zhurkin
Library Consultant: Kathleen Baxter
Production Specialist: Jane Klenk

Image Credits
Alamy: Chris Cooper-Smith, 14, Dave Stamboulis, 21, David Grossman, 8, Elisabeth
Peters, 15, Photos 12, 44; Capstone Studio/Karon Dubke, 42; Courtesy of James
Rocco, 43; Courtesy of Michele Byrd-McPhee, 12; Getty Images: AFP/Stan Honda,
22, Kevin Winter, 28; iStockphoto: Andreas Kermann, 11, 30, Elena Korenbaum, 40,
Scott Smith, 17, Soubrette, 33; Photo by J.J. Tiziou, 34; Shutterstock: A. Yakovlev,
cover, Anky, 31, Bill Florence, 5, Dana E. Fry, 18, Dragan Trifunovic, 41, Factoria
Singular Fotografia, 27, Henrique Daniel Araujo, 10, Kristian Sekulic, 37, Olga
Bogatyrenko, 19, Petro Feketa, 25, R. Gino Santa Maria, 4, 9, Ronald Sumners, back
cover (background texture) and throughout, Scott O. Smith, 6, Thomas Nord, 38,
Victor Newman, 23.

 This book was manufactured with paper containing
at least 10 percent post-consumer waste.

Library of Congress Cataloging-in-Publication Data
Fishkin, Rebecca, 1972–
    Dance : a practical guide to pursuing the art / by Rebecca
Love Fishkin ; reading adviser, Alexa L. Sandmann.
        p. cm. — (The performing arts)
    Includes bibliographical references and index.
    ISBN 978-0-7565-4363-1 (library binding)
    1. Dance—Juvenile literature. I. Title. II. Series.
    GV1596.5.F56 2011
    793.3—dc22   2010012605

Visit Compass Point Books on the Internet at *www.capstonepub.com*

TABLE OF CONTENTS

⭐ Introduction
You're a Dancer   p. 4

⭐ Chapter 1
Getting Started   p. 6

⭐ Chapter 2
Training   p. 14

⭐ Chapter 3
A Dancer's Tools   p. 22

⭐ Chapter 4
Preparing for Auditions   p. 28

⭐ Chapter 5
Realizing the Dream   p. 37

Glossary   p. 46

Additional Resources   p. 47

Index   p. 48

You're a Dancer

A dancer is an actor, an athlete, and a storyteller. From the classic grace of ballet to the contemporary energy of hip-hop, dance expresses the whole range of human emotions in order to entertain and communicate with an audience.

Dance is a constantly evolving art form. Ballet, for example, began in Italy in the 15th century but later was adopted by France, where it developed the positions and terms still used today. Modern dance rebelled against ballet's strictness to embrace free-form movement and elements of various styles. American jazz dancing grew out of African slave dances. Tap dancing can be dated back to Irish step, English clogging, and African dance movements. Hip-hop began in the streets of the Bronx, New York, and has become a youth-driven style that crosses socioeconomic and cultural barriers.

Swing, salsa, ballroom, Irish step, Latin, Flamenco, belly, country, break-dancing, and folk dancing—the styles are endless and constantly evolving. Today dancers stick to one style or mix elements of many to create their own expression.

As a dancer, there are many dance styles and traditions for you to explore.

To become a professional dancer, you need a strong mind and a strong body. Hours of practice will turn into years of hard work before you become a paid dancer on stage. Even more challenging are the competition and pressure that will follow you every step of the way.

Yet those stage lights shine brightly. If dancing is your dream, it is time to prepare for the journey ahead.

Chapter 1

Getting Started

Dancers can start as young as 4 or 5, and the first style they learn is often ballet. The positions and techniques of ballet are the foundation of many dance styles. Ballet helps young dancers develop good posture, timing, and grace, as well as an understanding of how movement and music work together.

Regardless of dance style, classes teach proper

technique and form. You will learn how to put steps together to music to form a routine and how to use your whole body to express a dance. If your studio has recitals, you will learn performance skills.

Look in the phone book or search the Web for classes offered by private studios, community centers, the YMCA, health clubs, and recreation centers. Ask your friends where they dance.

Compare prices, schedules, and class sizes. Find out whether a dance program specializes in one type of dance or many. Visit studios with an adult before signing up. Most instructors let you observe classes and may even let you take a free trial class. Ask instructors about their techniques and qualifications.

Examine the studio. It should be clean, well lit, and large enough to dance freely, with mirrors, barres, and a suitable floor (not concrete). Some serious dancers go to classes daily. Your studio should be a place you love—you should feel good when you

Starting Up

No matter how well you dance, starting a new class always presents new challenges. To become familiar with steps and technique, watch videos or read books about the type of dance you are learning.

Your dance studio should be a place where you feel happy and comfortable.

are there. Keep in mind, however, that as your dancing evolves, you may need to find a new studio or additional instruction to reach the next level.

Opportunities to perform exist outside your dance program as well. Your school may put on a musical with dancing. Your community may have a youth dance troupe. Theaters offer camps,

Dance High

Some cities have high schools that emphasize performing arts. They are an excellent first step to a dance career.

workshops, and youth productions. Well-known dance schools, colleges, and universities offer summer programs. Adult dance troupes also may offer youth opportunities.

In addition to classes and performing, immerse yourself in dance. Attend performances of all styles at theaters, street fairs, and other places. Rent dancing movies and watch music videos.

It may take time to discover what type of dancer you want to be. Even if you know which style you prefer, experiment by learning others. It will help you be certain what works best for you and will make it easier for you to be hired as a professional dancer.

Explore a variety of dance styles to expand your range and find the style that suits you best.

DANCING GEAR

Dancing requires special clothing and sometimes props to allow dancers to move comfortably and correctly. But before buying gear, ask your instructor about the studio's requirements. Much of the basic gear for ballet, jazz, and tap can be used for other styles. But the clothing and shoes are expensive, so take good care of your belongings.

Ballet: Ballet shoes are usually made of leather or canvas. Young dancers start with soft shoes that should fit snugly but have room to wiggle their toes. The more you dance, the more often you will have to replace your shoes. To make them last longer, never wear them outside, and always keep them clean.

Experienced ballet dancers wear pointe shoes, which have a hard toe for dancing on the tips of toes. Your teacher will tell you when you are ready for pointe shoes.

Ballerinas usually wear a leotard and tights, sometimes with short skirts or tutus. Male ballet dancers may wear tights, tight sweat pants, or shorts with tucked-in shirts. Try on an outfit before buying it. Do a few stretches to make sure it does not bunch or slip and that it allows you to move fully.

Jazz: Jazz dancers wear leotards and tights or jazz pants, which are lighter and tighter than sweat pants and vary in length. Jazz shoes are like ballet slippers with a heel. There are also jazz sneakers, which, like pointe shoes, have a hard toe.

Tap: Tap shoes have metal plates on the sole. The shoes come in many colors, but black, white, and beige are traditional. There are various styles and heel heights. The sound that tap shoes make is determined by the number of screws attached to the taps. Taps with three screws, called teletones, are the most common. Ask your teacher what you need.

When shopping for shoes, wear the type of socks or tights you will wear to dance. Avoid poorly fitting shoes and clothing. Dance gear is expensive. You will need to replace shoes and clothing regularly because of wear and size changes. You also will need costumes for recitals.

Michele Byrd-McPhee

Hip-Hop Dancer

Music and dance were an everyday part of life for young Michele Byrd-McPhee. Born in 1970 in Philadelphia, Pennsylvania, she danced with her family as they cleaned the house. Songs from her mother's extensive music collection blared from the speakers. At every family gathering, the children performed black social dances taught to them by Byrd-McPhee's mother, grandmother, aunts, and uncles.

In high school she became interested in street dance and clubs, where she found her calling: house dance, a style of dance that is influenced by African, Cuban, bebop, jazz, gospel, disco, and hip-hop movements and music. But dance did not become her first career. She earned a degree in community health studies. She became a social worker and later went into financial planning.

After a few years, Byrd-McPhee decided she really wanted to dance, so she left her career path to give it a try. She became well known as a club dancer in Philadelphia, and she became increasingly interested in the role of women in hip-hop dance. She was frustrated, however, because hip-hop offered women few training and performance opportunities.

In 1998 she teamed with another club dancer, Crystal Frazier, to empower women in hip-hop. They created Montäzh Performing Arts Company, an all-female hip-hop dance company. Montäzh PAC offers training, education, and performance opportunities, and it sponsors an annual hip-hop festival in Philadelphia.

In addition to her own dancing, choreography, and work at Montäzh PAC, Byrd-McPhee works with prominent hip-hop dancers, including Buddha Stretch, to create opportunities for dancers. Byrd-McPhee also enhanced her professional skills by earning a master's degree in arts administration.

"Since I never did the little-girl-dance-class thing, I never thought of myself as a dancer, even though I performed alongside trained dancers and held my own," she says. "I began to see my talents … instead of focusing on what I did not have as a dancer, I focused on what I did have."

Byrd-McPhee recommends that young dancers train in many styles, as well as in other art forms. The more a dancer understands art, the more he or she brings to the stage.

She also tells young dancers to choose their teachers wisely. Make sure their training is extensive and thorough, because instructors create a student's foundation for a dancing future. And remember, dancing is a long-term commitment. Studying, practicing, and educating yourself is full-time work—you cannot let yourself be distracted, she says.

"There will always be obstacles, doubt, or life changes that put in question your commitment," she says. "Be prepared to go around, reassure yourself, and get back on track when all those things happen. A great sense of self keeps you grounded and gives you a place to go back to when this business gets crazy."

Chapter 2

Training

Like athletes, dancers must prepare their bodies for demanding workouts. Insufficient training leads to injury and prevents you from becoming the best dancer you can be.

Dancers need excellent posture. Good posture is important for strength, flexibility, and injury prevention. When you are standing correctly, you should be able to imagine a straight line passing from the top of your head through your spine to your feet. Your weight should be distributed evenly across the soles of your feet, and your feet should be a little less than hip-width apart. Do not lock your knees. Let your arms hang loosely at your sides, and relax your shoulders. Your head should be level and square on your neck.

Maintain your posture as you stretch and dance. This will help you do the moves correctly and will make your body look more graceful. Strive for good posture while walking and sitting.

Dancers also need strong abdominal muscles. Try abdominal curls to build strength. Lie on your back on a mat or rug with your knees bent and your feet flat on the floor. Rest your hands on the outer parts of your thighs.

Back bridges will help increase your flexibility.

Pull in your abdomen, and tighten your buttocks and the inner parts of your thighs. Then curl up slowly using the abdominal muscles. As you curl, slide your hands down your thighs until your fingertips touch your kneecaps. Your waist should stay on the floor, while your head, neck, and shoulders lift. Hold for a minute, release, and repeat. Other abdominal exercises include pelvic tilts, back bridges, and twists.

It is important to strengthen your ankles and calves. For a simple ankle exercise, write your name with your foot, without moving your leg. Sit on a chair, point your toes, and use your ankle to spell your name in the air. Make large and small letters. To work your calves, stand on the balls of your feet with your ankles parallel, about shoulder width apart. With a straight body and head, rise as far as

Do Your Homework

From warm-ups to advanced dance steps, you can find information about almost anything you want to know in books, magazines, and on the Internet. Before trying anything new, consult your teacher or a more experienced dancer to make sure the exercises are right for you and that you are doing them correctly.

you can on your toes. Keep the back of your legs firm. Hold and repeat the exercise until you've done it 10 times.

Even if you are not a ballet dancer, learn to do a proper plié and use it to build knee strength and flexibility. Bring your heels together with your toes pointing in opposite directions and your feet flat. Bend at the knee, keeping your knees over your toes, with a straight back and neck. Practice small knee bends (demi plié) and deep bends (grand plié).

Pliés are an excellent way to build knee strength and flexibility.

Dancers need excellent stamina. They can spend eight or more hours a day in class, rehearsal, and performance. Additional cardiovascular activities, such as swimming, biking, or walking, can build stamina. Talk with your dance instructors to choose the best exercise, and do not overdo it.

Always warm up and cool down. Many young dancers injure themselves by leaping into a full workout without a sufficient warm-up. Proper stretching before and after

Swimming is an excellent way to strengthen your heart and body.

dancing is important for a dancer to fully execute steps
and to avoid injury.

Listen to your body. Treat minor problems before
they become major injuries. Repetitive movements and
long workouts often lead to tendinitis, ankle sprains, and
injuries of the back, hips, knees, hamstrings, and feet. If
you are injured, tell your teacher, who can help you correct
your technique to keep the injury from recurring. Make
sure to see a doctor as well. It will be tempting to resume
your practice routine when the pain lessens, but returning
too soon can result in permanent damage.

Besides training your body, you need to develop an ear
for music. Dance and music are partners in a performance.
Your routines will be choreographed so you will move in

Strong and Stress-Free

Take a yoga or a Pilates class to build strength and flexibility. You will learn good breathing and meditation techniques, which you can use to calm yourself and focus before performances.

time with the musical accompaniment. If your movements are off-tempo, you will get ahead of the other dancers or fall behind them.

Practice moving to the beat of a song. Choose a favorite song, and tap your right foot to the strong beats and your left to the downbeats. Let your arms swing. Now start moving in small steps. Then add your body. When you truly feel the rhythm, the dance will look like natural movements, not just choreographed steps.

Let the rhythm of the music flow through your body and guide your movements.

WARM UP, STRETCH, AND COOL DOWN

Dancers need to be limber to execute dance moves properly and to prevent injury. Your instructor will provide an appropriate warm-up routine and will keep you stretching throughout class. You also can add the following basic stretches to your routine:

Always begin stretching slowly, because your muscles will be cold. Many dancers start with their necks and backs and then move down the body. Stand straight and do gentle neck rolls. Roll your shoulders forward and backward, then raise and lower them. Extend your arms to the sides and roll them in both directions. Bring your hands together in front of you, entwine your fingers, turn your palms out, and stretch your arms. Repeat behind your back (palms facing in). Gently arch your back backward, then bend forward, bringing your arms with clasped hands slowly over your head.

Stretch your sides by lifting one arm at a time overhead and bending in the direction your hand is pointing. Then bend forward and let your neck and arms hang to stretch your spine. Keep your hips level and straight.

Sit cross-legged and bend over your legs to stretch your hips. While sitting, straighten your legs in front, flex your feet, and reach over your legs to stretch your hamstrings. Keep your back flat. Spread your legs and stretch forward again,

Splits are a good warm-up exercise.

trying to bring your chest to the floor. Stretch over each leg, hands reaching toward your feet. Do splits on each side.

Always do cool-down exercises, and stretch again after dancing. Your muscles will be warm, so you will be able to stretch farther and more thoroughly during this time.

Move slowly and gently through your stretches. Do not force a stretch, and remember that you will feel more limber on some days than others. Breathe while you stretch, and repeat each stretch at least twice. Add some light stretching to your nondancing activities. A few minutes in the morning and at night (maybe while you watch television) can improve your overall flexibility.

Chapter 3

A Dancer's Tools

Talent will take you a long way, but a professional dancer needs much more than that. Dancing is thrilling, exhausting, and highly competitive, and if you are to succeed, you need to develop certain personal qualities as well.

Dancers need discipline. Dancing is rigorous work, with long workdays, low wages, and intense pressure. You need discipline to learn precise movements and complicated choreography, and to train your body to dance correctly and expressively.

Self-discipline will help you balance dancing with school and a growing social life. Social pressures at school and in the dance studio can be confusing and complicated. Setting priorities will allow you to choose when to spend time with others and when outside activities are distracting you from your training.

If you have a deep-down desire to dance, you will go further than most. Many dancers who start young drop out when the work gets hard, even if they love dancing.

Successful dancers don't just love to dance; they need to dance.

You may not discover what type of dancer you are until high school, or even later, and at times the work may seem too hard. But the serious dancers—the ones who stick it out—are the ones who make it.

Physically, dancers must be agile, coordinated, and graceful, with a good sense of tempo and artistic expression. They need physical and mental stamina. Their bodies must be fit and limber to withstand the lessons and performances. But mental factors are just as important. Your mind must be engaged to memorize choreography. You also have to develop emotional strength to deal with the pressures of dancing.

Many dancers are perfectionists. They demand much from others, but even more from themselves. This sense of urgency and seriousness can help a dancer reach great heights, but it also can lead to frustration, depression, and injury. Dancers of every age and ability must cope with rejection. If your image and technique

Mentor Me!

Find a mentor, such as an instructor you admire or an experienced dancer. A mentor can give you individual attention and support to guide you through the difficult process of becoming a dancer.

do not fit the vision of an artistic director, you will not get a role, no matter how well you dance or how hard you try. This happens repeatedly throughout a dancing career. A professional dancer must develop the confidence to bounce back after an unsuccessful audition.

Dance is an art form, but it is also an athletic activity. As an athlete, you need to exercise both body and mind to be a successful competitor. As an artist,

Not all auditions will be successful, but what will make you successful is your ability to learn from failure and bounce back.

you need to turn your love of dance into a product you can sell to an audience. It is a difficult journey, but the proper tools make the task a bit easier.

HEALTHY BODY, HEALTHY DANCER

Teenagers' bodies change dramatically in a short time. Growth spurts affect agility and balance. Hormonal changes affect the body and the emotions. What your body looks like at age 9 is very different from how it looks at 16.

A dancer's body is his or her most important tool. The lines and shape of your body become part of the expression of the dance. There is no changing the fact that body type is important for dancers. The effects of puberty on your body can be upsetting. You may begin to worry too much about your weight, height, and shape—especially as you watch yourself every day in the studio mirrors.

Obsessing about body changes can lead to poor self-esteem and eating problems, which can turn into health problems that weaken your body. They can become so severe that you can no longer dance. It is important to realize, and accept the fact, that no matter what you do, you cannot change your body type.

What you can do is develop healthful habits. This means making sure you get good nutrition, adequate sleep, and exercise. It means no unhealthful dieting or fasting. It means no smoking, drinking, or drugs. It means talking to an adult you can trust if you begin to worry too much about your body.

A balanced diet is very important to staying strong and well. Eating provides the energy you need to dance. Eat a variety of lean proteins, fruits, vegetables, and whole grains. Avoid saturated fats and too much sugar. Eat enough calories to sustain yourself through workouts, and drink plenty of water. Always eat breakfast. If your schedule does not allow for three meals, eat small meals during the day.

If you establish good habits as a young dancer, you will get through your natural body transformations in a healthy way. The result will be the best body you can have.

A healthy, balanced diet will help you develop a strong dancer's body.

Chapter 4

Preparing for Auditions

Auditions are a way of life for dancers. Every new role or show starts with one. Young dancers face their first auditions as teenagers when trying out for scholarships and dance companies. Thorough preparation is the best way to do well. Make sure you know the rules and requirements of the audition, as well as exactly where to go and when and how to get there.

Dance auditions often require you to perform a specific routine, which you may have to learn at the audition rather than in advance. Make sure you have a good view of the instructor. You need to see the instructor clearly to learn the steps. Concentrate on absorbing the movements.

If you are allowed to prepare your own routine, choose expressive music and movements that show your strengths. An audition is not the time to experiment. Your costume should fit well and accentuate your body but be appropriate to the audition. If you can choose your costume, wear something that makes you feel good.

Practice until you know the routine. If you get tired or discouraged, take a day off.

Pack your audition supplies the night before. You will need shoes, a costume, makeup, hair clips, a first-aid kit, a needle and thread, moleskin for blisters, a résumé, a photo or video, and water.

Audition in Style

An audition will rarely call for only one style of dance. Learn as many types as possible. This will help you learn combinations faster and ensure that you are ready for whatever the choreographer has designed.

Get a good night's sleep. About three hours before the audition, eat a light meal with some protein. Stay hydrated, and avoid sugar and caffeine.

Arrive with plenty of time to breathe, stretch, and warm up. When you take the stage, smile, make eye contact, and be positive. Do not look at your feet. Put emotion into your routine and show how much you love to dance.

Take feedback seriously, especially from instructors

Eye contact and a smile will help you connect with your audience.

Ballroom dancers participate in competitions, which require preparation and focus similar to auditions.

and experienced dancers, who know what it takes to succeed. It can be difficult to hear a negative review, but use it to improve. The best way to get better at auditions is to keep trying.

CALMING THE JITTERS

Auditions, recitals, and other performances are stressful. Even professional dancers experience some anxiety before performing. Stage fright can cause a dry mouth, sweating, shakiness, nausea, and a rapid heartbeat. The more important the audition or performance, the scarier it can be.

Preparation is crucial to overcoming nerves. It will make you more confident that you know your choreography and timing. Making a checklist of what you need to bring and do before the audition or show also helps.

Just before taking the stage, do a few full body stretches. (You should already have warmed up.) Close your eyes and think calming thoughts. Take deep, slow breaths and visualize a successful performance. Keep yourself focused on the dance.

Some dancers find that sharing light conversation or swapping shoulder massages helps calm nerves. Others need a few quiet minutes alone. Professional dancers develop all sorts of ways to reduce the jitters, from certain warm-up routines to meditation to good-luck charms.

If you find that your nervousness does not subside once you start dancing, and if it hurts your performance, talk to your instructors. They can recommend techniques or coaches to help you learn to cope with your performance anxiety. Don't forget: The audience members are there to share your love of dance. They want to enjoy themselves. You should too.

Learn what stretches relax you, and do them before you step on stage.

Amy Smith

Improvisational Dancer

Like many girls, a 6-year-old Amy Smith started dancing with ballet. By age 12, her teachers in Ann Arbor, Michigan, recognized her talent and tried to persuade her to attend ballet boarding school. But Smith knew she would not become a ballerina, so she branched out into jazz and tap. As a student at Wesleyan University, Smith planned to become a lawyer or college professor. She took classes in modern dance, but dance was just going to be a hobby—until she discovered choreography and improvisation. Smith was hooked and started to rethink her life as a dance artist.

After college Smith spent a year with the Center for New Dance Development in the Netherlands. Knowing she wanted to perform and create contemporary dance theater, Smith teamed up with like-minded dancers David Brick and Andrew

Simonet in 1993 to create the Headlong Dance Theater in Philadelphia, Pennsylvania.

"We wanted somewhere we could work day jobs part time to support our dance work, have our own studio, and just make tons of dances," Smith said. "We got good at making dances, and we slowly and surely built up our community of audience members and fellow artists."

At Headlong, Smith and her co-directors create dances that reflect and comment on contemporary culture. They incorporate ballet, jazz, tap, and modern dance, and combine dance with gestures and techniques from theater, sports, and even sign language. Headlong has created and performed more than 40 dances around the world. In 1999 the company won a "Bessie" (New York Dance and Performance Award) for its piece *ST*R W*RS.*

Headlong participates actively in the Philadelphia dance community and offers an educational program for young dance artists. The Headlong Performance Institute brings college students and recent college graduates to Philadelphia for an intensive semester of dance instruction and performance. Participants earn academic credit from Bryn Mawr College.

Smith counsels young dancers to improve their performance skills by taking classes in improvisation, theater, clowning, and commedia dell'arte. "Learning basic compositional skills and being able to talk and use your face in performance will make you a much more appealing performer to many choreographers," she says.

She advises dancers to build an understanding of basic anatomy. Learning about the hips, knees, ankles, and corresponding muscles—how they work together and how to move them properly—can help a dancer perform longer and more safely.

Balancing a dance career with outside interests and family is not easy. In addition to her work with Headlong and raising two children, Smith serves on the board of trustees for Dance/USA and helps artists with tax preparation and financial planning. Being a part of a community is key to surviving the challenges of the dance world.

"Find like-minded artists you can work with wherever they are. Making a living wage as a dancer is near impossible, so find a day job you can live with and that will sustain your dance work," Smith says. "Be yourself. Don't even try to fit into the boxes ... demanded by most of your teachers. Your intelligence and idiosyncratic [unique] movement style is your greatest gift as a dance artist."

The dance industry is loaded with competition and
rejection. There are only so many open spots, and the
fight for roles is fierce. And dancing cannot always be a
full-time job. Many major companies hire by the season
or by the show. When the show ends, dancers need new

jobs. Some shows pay only for one performance at a time.

Many professional dancers spend their careers in the corps, the group of dancers whose performance supports the lead dancers. Lead roles and solo spots are the most coveted and most difficult to get. Some shows, such as the Rockettes of Radio City Music Hall in New York City, are mostly corps performances.

Beyond the stage, dancers find roles in television, movies, and music videos. These roles, too, are highly competitive.

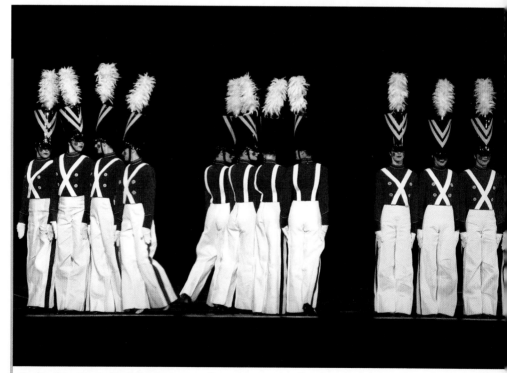

Radio City Music Hall Rockettes perform in costume for their annual Christmas Extravaganza.

Dancing is an expensive art, and wages can be low and irregular. Dancers usually need other employment to support themselves between shows. Some shows require dancers to buy their own costumes. Dancers also need to replace gear constantly.

Apprenticeships

Some dance companies have apprenticeships that give young dancers training before they are offered paid stage roles. This is a great way to gain experience, meet dancers, and learn the culture of a company.

Eventually all dancers need an offstage job. As early as age 30, a dancer's body begins to lose the flexibility and endurance needed to withstand the brutal workouts of daily dancing. An injury can end a performance career at any time. Every dancer—no matter what level—needs a backup plan.

Consider getting a college degree in a field not directly related to dance, such as teaching or business. It can help you find a second career to earn money either while you dance or after you retire. You can pursue a second degree while studying dance, though the demands of your training may make this challenging. Many dancers return to school after they stop performing.

DANCE COMPANY OR DANCING SCHOOL?

As you grow older and more focused about your goals, you may have a decision to make: Should you study dance at a college or join a dance company? Both provide rigorous training with qualified instructors and talented peers, but there are major differences.

When you join a dance company, you become a paid dancer. You train and perform within the company. Companies have specific goals and approaches. They do not provide education in subjects other than dance.

If your focus is ballet, joining a company may be a smart move. Many ballet companies want to bring dancers on as teenagers. Older dancers may face tougher competition. Companies specializing in other dance styles may be more flexible. It is important to research various dance companies to

find out what kind of dancers they are looking for and whether and when you would qualify. You should always watch a company perform before joining.

To join a company, you must audition. You will need a detailed résumé listing all of your training and experience, including honors, roles, workshops, and competitions. You will need to make a video of yourself dancing. If the company likes your submission, you will be invited to audition. Acceptance into major dance companies is highly competitive. Lesser-known companies also offer excellent training and opportunities and are easier to join.

College provides a broader educational background. You can earn a degree in dance or performance arts while taking general education courses. You also can pursue studies that may boost your dancing career. For example, a business degree could help you open your own dance studio. A physical therapy degree could help you become a dance therapist. You can perform in school productions. If you have time, you can take additional courses outside the college.

Many former dancers continue in the dance field by teaching the next generation of dancers once their own performing careers are over.

Think about what you can do with your love of dance other than dancing. You can teach or perhaps open your own studio. You can become a choreographer or an artistic director with a theater. You can be a dance therapist. You could even design your own line of dancewear.

There may be no denying those stage lights. To get there, you will work harder and longer than you ever imagined. If you stay healthy and focused, you *can* do the work. You may begin with baby steps, but eventually you will start leaping toward your dreams.

James Rocco

Dancer, Choreographer, and Producer

James Rocco's family thought dancing would be just a hobby for him. It did not take long, however, for Rocco to prove he was destined for a life on, and behind, the stage.

Rocco was fascinated by the moves he saw on the streets of his native New York City. He realized he could combine his love of rock and roll with dance in an athletic, energetic style that was suited for musical theater.

Rocco began tap dancing with a children's group, and at age 12 he went on tour with the musical *Oliver!* He began to pick up choreography by observing the actions of choreographers and by analyzing dance on film. He directed his first show in New York City at the age of 16 at The Lambs Theatre.

As an adult Rocco landed on Broadway with a role as Rum Tum Tugger in the musical *Cats*. His first break as a director and choreographer came when he appeared in a production of *Jesus Christ Superstar* at the Paper Mill Playhouse in Millburn, New Jersey. At the request of the producers, he took over a remounting of the show. That led to his being asked to direct and choreograph more than 50 major musicals in the United States and abroad, including *Grey Gardens*, *The Sound of Music*, *The Rocky Horror Show*,

Sweeney Todd, *Joseph and the Amazing Technicolor Dreamcoat*, and *Cabaret*. He also has directed the Japanese television and stage production *Galaxy Express 999* and *The World We Create*, a TV documentary that received a regional Emmy nomination.

In 1995, while working at the Lyric Theatre of Oklahoma, Rocco produced *Broadway Sings for the Heartland*, a benefit to support victims of the Oklahoma City bombing, with stars from across the country.

Rocco says one of the career achievements he is proudest of is re-envisioning the Broadway version of *Singin' in the Rain* with the Music Theatre of Wichita in 1990.

"I could see it on stage as an homage to the art of performance and to the people who

Rocco adapted dances from the film version of Singin' in the Rain *for his production.*

express themselves through song and dance," he says.

Rocco's version was a success. He has staged productions of the musical across the United States and a Japanese version in Tokyo.

Rocco is the vice president for programming and producing artistic director at the Ordway Center for the Performing Arts in St. Paul, Minnesota. He books and produces traveling Broadway shows.

Rocco tells the many young dancers he works with that moving comfortably is not the only element of good dancing. He advises them to study the masters through film and video to learn the evolution of dance, and to become more aware of how shape and line define the art.

"Your body is your tool," he says. "It takes discipline to keep that tool sharp. The dancers who survive are the ones who learn the history of dance and the ones who understand their bodies."

Rocco has learned that, as much as dancers would like to, they cannot spend all their time being creative. One of his greatest challenges has been learning that he must also be a businessperson and salesperson to survive as an artist. He tells young dancers that they must constantly seek out new opportunities.

"Become aware of the roles you are appropriate for and continue to find ways to expand that list of roles," he says. "All of your marketing materials should capture the true you and the best you. We are all in the business of telling stories. Know where and how you would fit best when telling a story."

GLOSSARY

barres horizontal handrails used for balance at a dance studio

cardiovascular relating to or involving the heart and blood vessels

choreography steps and patterns of a dance

commedia dell'arte form of improvisational performance that features masked performers acting out sketches largely without scripts or choreography

dance company formal organization of dancers who train and perform together; usually specializes in one style of dance

dance therapist person who helps others use movement to improve their mental and physical health

improvisation creating a new performance on the spot

Pilates exercise regimen typically performed with the use of specialized equipment

plié basic ballet knee bend

props items that a performer needs to carry or use

recital public dance performance, often held by dance studios to display students' skills

résumé brief list of a person's jobs, education, and awards

Rockettes dance company of Radio City Music Hall, in New York City, known for precision chorus line productions

stamina strength or endurance to withstand illness or fatigue

tendinitis inflammation of a tendon, the connective tissue that joins muscle with bone

yoga system of exercises and meditation that helps people become mentally relaxed and physically fit

READ MORE

Anderson, Janet. *Modern Dance*. New York: Chelsea House, 2010.

Bussell, Darcey, and Patricia Linton. *The Ballet Book*. New York: DK, 2006.

Feinstein, Stephen. *Savion Glover*. Berkeley Heights, N.J.: Enslow Publishers, 2009.

McAlpine, Margaret. *Working in Music and Dance*. Milwaukee, Wis.: Gareth Stevens Pub., 2006.

Nathan, Amy. *Meet the Dancers: From Ballet, Broadway, and Beyond*. New York: Henry Holt, 2008.

INTERNET SITES

FactHound offers a safe, fun way to find Internet sites related to this book. All of the sites on FactHound have been researched by our staff.

Here's all you do:

Visit *www.facthound.com*

Type in this code: 9780756543631

INDEX

abdominal muscles, 15–16
ankle exercises, 16
anxiety, 32
apprenticeships, 39
auditions, 25, 28–31, 32, 41

ballet, 4–5, 6–7, 10, 40–41
body types, 26
Brick, David, 34
Byrd-McPhee, Michele, 12–13

calf exercises, 16–17
choreography, 18–19, 22, 24, 32, 43–44
clogging, 5
clothing. See costumes.
competition, 5, 22, 37, 38, 40, 41
confidence, 25, 32
corps performances, 38
costumes, 10, 11, 29, 39

dance companies, 12–13, 28, 35, 37–38, 39, 40–41
dance studios, 7–8, 10, 23, 41, 42
degrees, 39, 41
demi plié, 17
discipline, 22–23, 45

education, 6–9, 13, 35, 36, 39, 40, 41
exercises, 15–17, 19, 20–21, 25, 26
expenses, 10–11, 39

feedback, 31
flexibility, 14–15, 17, 19, 21, 39, 40
focus, 19, 32, 42
Frazier, Crystal, 12

grand plié, 17

Headlong Dance Theater, 35
hip-hop dancing, 4, 5, 12–13
house dance, 12

injuries, 14, 17–18, 20, 24, 39

jazz dancing, 5, 10, 11
job opportunities, 13, 37–38, 41, 42, 45

mentors, 24
modern dance, 4–5
Montäzh Performing Arts Company, 12–13
music, 6, 7, 18–19, 29
musicals, 8, 43–45

nutrition, 26–27, 30

perfectionism, 24
plié, 17
posture, 6, 14–15

recitals, 7, 11, 32
rejection, 24–25, 37
résumés, 29, 41
rhythm. See tempo.
Rocco, James, 43–45
routines, 7, 18–19, 20, 29, 30, 32

shoes, 10, 11, 29
side jobs, 39
Simonet, Andrew, 34–35
Smith, Amy, 34–36
Stretch, Buddha, 13
stretching, 10, 15, 17–18, 20–21, 30, 32
styles, 5, 6, 9, 10, 12, 13, 29, 40

tap dancing, 5, 10, 11
tempo, 19, 24
timing, 6, 32

wages, 22, 36, 39, 40
warm-up exercises, 17–18, 20–21, 30, 32

About the Author

Rebecca Love Fishkin has written for newspapers, magazines, and Web sites, as well as books for young readers. She has managed an early literacy program and worked in the communications department of an international nonprofit organization that repairs children's cleft lips and palates. She lives in Lawrenceville, New Jersey.